OCTONAUTS™

and the Electric Torpedo Rays

The daring crew of the Octopod are ready to embark on an exciting new mission!

INKLING OCTOPUS
(Professor)

KWAZII CAT
(Lieutenant)

PESO PENGUIN
(Medic)

BARNACLES BEAR
(Captain)

TWEAK BUNNY
(Engineer)

SHELLINGTON SEA OTTER
(Field Researcher)

DASHI DOG
(Photographer)

TUNIP THE VEGIMAL
(Ship's Cook)

EXPLORE . RESCUE . PROTECT

OCTONAUTS™

and the Electric Torpedo Rays

SIMON AND SCHUSTER

"Full speed ahead, Dashi," ordered Captain Barnacles. The Octopod rushed through the ocean – it was on a tight schedule today!

"My friend Sandy the sea turtle always swims through these waters at this time of year," said Tweak. "I hope we get there in time to see her."

Barnacles showed Tweak a radar picture of a
deep undersea canyon.

  "Sandy should be just on the other side," he smiled.
"We'll be there faster than you can say 'buncha muncha
crunchy . . .' oh!"

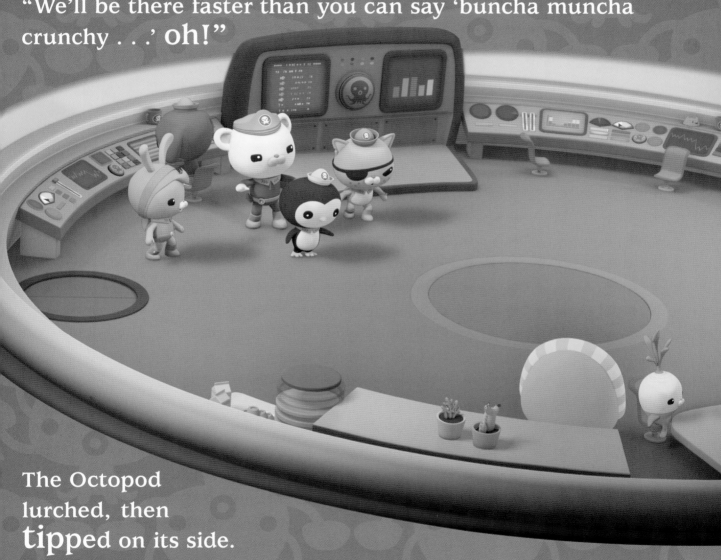

The Octopod
lurched, then
tipped on its side.

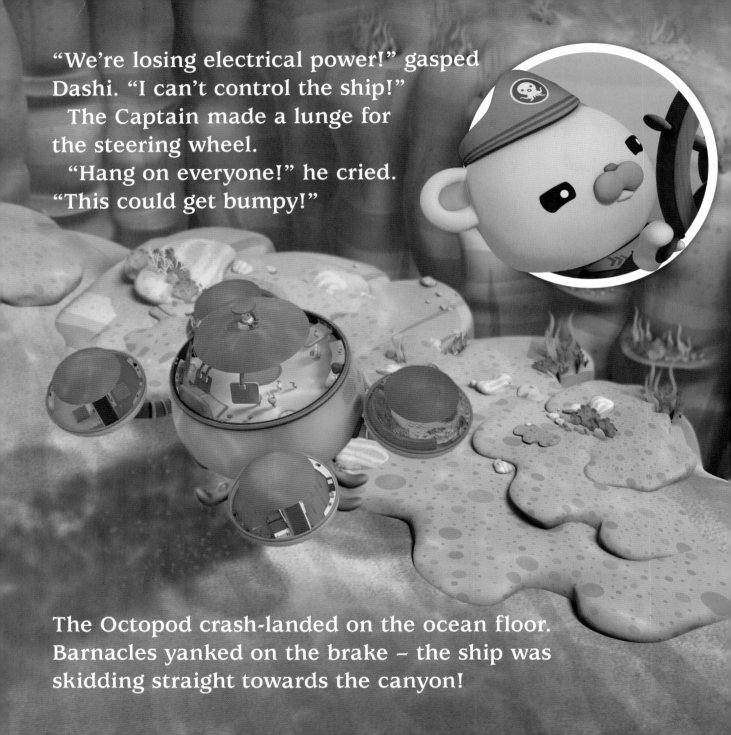

"We're losing electrical power!" gasped Dashi. "I can't control the ship!"

The Captain made a lunge for the steering wheel.

"Hang on everyone!" he cried. "This could get bumpy!"

The Octopod crash-landed on the ocean floor. Barnacles yanked on the brake – the ship was skidding straight towards the canyon!

The Octopod screeched to a stop millimetres away from the canyon edge.

"Shiver me whiskers!" yowled Kwazii. "That was a close one!"

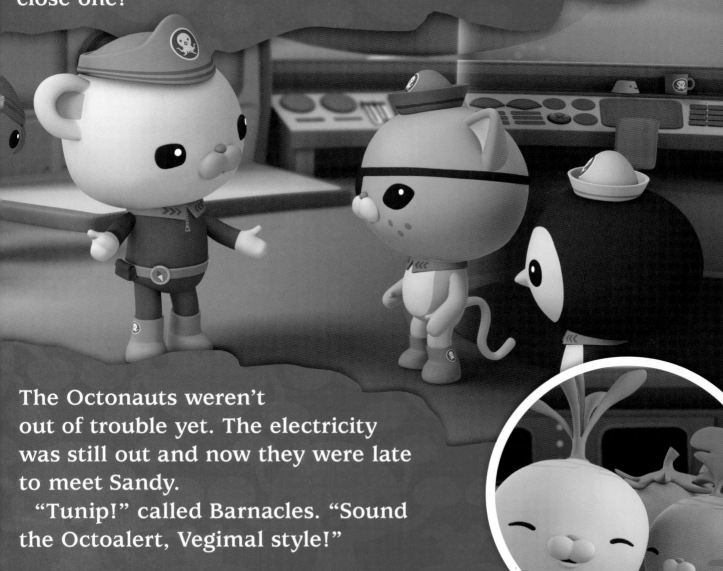

The Octonauts weren't out of trouble yet. The electricity was still out and now they were late to meet Sandy.

"Tunip!" called Barnacles. "Sound the Octoalert, Vegimal style!"

"Octonauts, to

the launch **bay!**"

"I think I found the problem, Cap'!" announced Tweak. "The ship's battery is completely out of electricity! Without power, the Octopod won't work. Even the Octohatch is jammed."

"We better check that the ship isn't damaged on the outside," decided Barnacles. "Kwazii, Peso, activate helmets!"

The Octopod was in a dangerous situation.

"It could fall into the canyon at any minute," frowned Peso.

The crew set to work tying the ship down.

The job was done in no time.

"Now there's nothing to worry about," announced Kwazii. "The Octopod's as secure as . . .

yeeeoooOOWWWW!"

A freckled fish had **zapped** Kwazii!
   "What's the big idea, stepping on my tail like that?" he snapped.

"We didn't mean to startle you," said Captain Barnacles. "How did you do that?"
   "I'm an electric torpedo ray," replied the stranger. "That was a little warning zap, but I can make big zaps of electricity too."
   Barnacles grinned. The ray had just sparked an amazing idea.

🐙 FACT: ELECTRICITY

The ray has a special part inside its body that makes electricity.

The Octonauts led the ray up to the Launch Bay. When Barnacles explained his plan, Tweak connected a wire to the ship's battery. If their new friend could zap the wire, it would recharge the battery and give the Octopod back its power!

"I might just get to see Sandy after all," grinned Tweak. "Stand clear!" called the Captain. "Electricity is dangerous!" The ray closed his eyes and prepared to zap . . . but **nothing** happened.

"I guess I can only make really big zaps when something scares me or when I'm eating," sighed the ray.

Just then, Tunip waddled in with a tray of fish biscuits.

Whoops!

Tunip tripped over, sending biscuits splashing into the water. The ray dived for a snack. Suddenly a jolt of electricity powered up the wire!

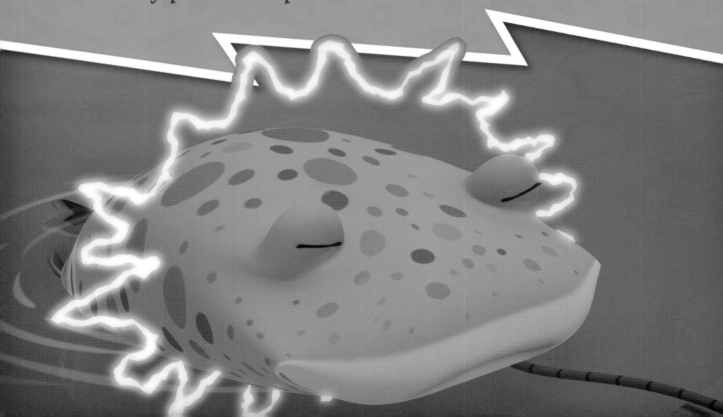

The lights flickered on for an instant, but the ray's spark was too weak.

"Do you have any friends that could help?" asked Barnacles.

The ray nodded. If he could make enough electricity to light up a whole room, a group of rays might be able to recharge the Octopod!

The Vegimals started loading biscuits onto the wire. There wasn't a second to lose!

The Octonauts carefully lowered the snack-studded wire out through the Octohatch, following it down to the seabed.

"Come on, guys!" called the electric torpedo ray. "Dinner is served."

Within seconds, the ocean was teeming with hungry rays. One by one, they started blasting the fish biscuits, sending shocks back up the wire.

"It's working!" cried Peso.

Soon the Octopod's battery was full again! The Octonauts
cheered, but the rays kept on feeding and zapping.

"Watch it!" shouted one.

"Get out of my way!" yelled another.

The rays were pushing and shoving so hard, the ropes
holding the ship started to quiver.

The Octopod's ropes
s‑t‑r‑e‑t‑c‑h‑e‑d,
then snapped!

"Sorry!" shouted the
rays, as the Octopod
tumbled into the canyon.

"I've got to get to the
controls!" bellowed
Barnacles.

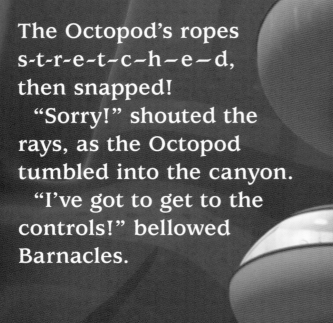

The Captain dived into the
darkness, but the Octopod
was slipping out of sight!

"Looks as if you could use
a lift!" said a friendly voice.
Sandy had turned up at just

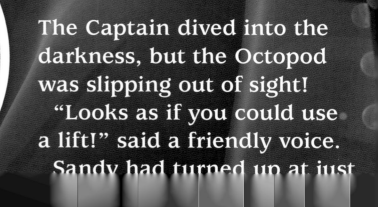

Barnacles hopped onto the sea turtle's back. Sandy plunged after the ship, bringing the pair level with the Octohatch.

"You'll have to jump for it!" Sandy cried.

Barnacles summoned all his polar bear strength. It was now or never . . .

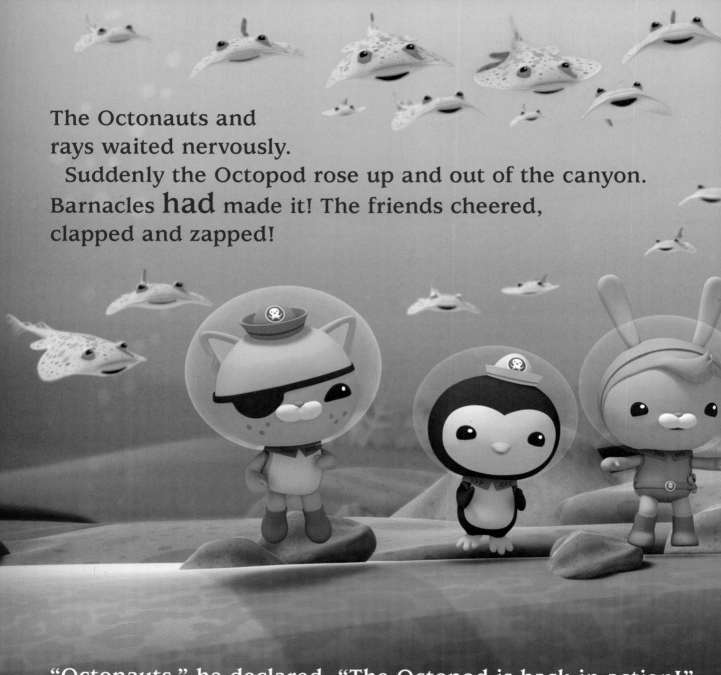

The Octonauts and rays waited nervously.

Suddenly the Octopod rose up and out of the canyon. Barnacles **had** made it! The friends cheered, clapped and zapped!

"Octonauts," he declared. "The Octopod is back in action!"

Tweak and Sandy gave each other a happy high five.
   "Thanks for coming all this way to see me," smiled the sea turtle. "I hope it wasn't too much trouble."

Barnacles looked up at the bumped and battered Octopod.
   "Err, not too much trouble Sandy!" he grinned, bursting into chuckles.

Calling all Octonauts! Our mission to meet Sandy introduced us to a shocking new friend – the electric torpedo ray. This curious creature can be hard to spot, but when it jolts into action, sparks fly!

FACT FILE: THE ELECTRIC TORPEDO RAY

The electric torpedo ray has a flat, speckled back. It makes electric shocks to zap food or other fish.

- It lives in shallow water.
- It eats fish.

OCTOFACTS:

1. The torpedo ray gives out a warning zap if it feels scared.

2. It also creates sparks when it gets hungry.

3. The ray likes to bury itself in the sand during the day.

Dive into action with these super, splashtastic Octonauts books!

Ready for Action in the GUP – A!

and the Giant Squid

Meet the Crew

and the Decorator Crab

and the Electric Torpedo Rays

and the Whale Shark

WWW.THEOCTONAUTS.COM

www.simonandschuster.co.uk

OCTONAUTS™

and the Electric Torpedo Rays

The crew are travelling to meet Tweak's old pal Sandy
when disaster strikes – the Octopod gets a power failure!
Only a very special type of sea creature can put the
spark back into Tweak's mission.
Octonauts, let's do this!

BARNACLES   **KWAZII**   **PESO**   **SHELLINGTON**   **INKLING**   **TWEAK**   **DASHI**   **TUNIP**

EXPLORE . RESCUE . PROTECT

WWW.THEOCTONAUTS.COM

SIMON AND SCHUSTER
First published in Great Britain in 2011 by Simon and Schuster UK Ltd
1st Floor, 222 Grays Inn Road, London WC1X 8HB
A CBS Company

ISBN 978-0-85707-340-2
Printed in China
10 9 8 7 6 5 4 3 2 1
www.simonandschuster.co.uk

chorion

SIMON
AND
SCHUSTER

£4.99

ISBN 978-0-85707-340-2

9 780857 073402

FSC
www.fsc.org
MIX
Paper from
responsible sources
FSC® C104723